A STORY ABOUT CHANGE

Moving Day
for Sam

BY PAMELA KENNEDY

ILLUSTRATED BY

ANTON PETROV

gp Kids℠

Nashville, Tennessee

ISBN-13: 978-0-8249-5558-8

Published by GPKids
An imprint of Ideals Publications
A Guideposts Company
535 Metroplex Drive, Suite 250
Nashville, Tennessee 37211
www.idealsbooks.com

Color separations by Precision Color Graphics, Franklin, Wisconsin
Printed and bound in Italy by LEGO

Library of Congress Cataloging-in-Publication Data

Kennedy, Pamela, 1946-
  Moving day for Sam / written by Pamela Kennedy ; illustrated by Anton Petrov.
     p. cm.
  Summary: Sam is unhappy and afraid when his parents announce they will be moving across the country to California, but his mother prays with him, his brother helps make the drive fun, and his new home and school turn out to be just fine.
  ISBN-13: 978-0-8249-5558-8 (alk. paper)
  ISBN-10: 0-8249-5558-7 (alk. paper)
  [1. Moving, Household--Fiction. 2. Lost and found possessions--Fiction. 3. Family life--Fiction. 4. Christian life--Fiction.] I. Petrov, Anton, ill. II. Title.
  PZ7.K3849Mov 2007
  [E]--dc22
                        2006101587

10 9 8 7 6 5 4 3 2 1

Designed by Eve DeGrie

For Josh, Doug, and Anne who learned, through many moves, that home is truly where your heart is. —P.J.K.

There's no place like home. —A.P.

A Note to Parents
By Vicki Wiley

We're moving! These words can create a lot of emotions in all of us; we can be excited and very anxious at the same time. Children have their own reactions when faced with a move: excitement, curiosity, sadness, and fear. When planning a move, remember that your young children are looking to you to decide how they will feel. If you show stress or have difficulty with the move, they may echo your feelings.

Some ideas for helping children cope:

* Discuss the move with your children. Let them know where you are moving. Make it fun and interesting for the children by working together to find information about the new location at the library or online. Explain why you are moving. If the move is due to a major change, such as a divorce or death, be thoughtful about what you say.

* Pray with your children. Choose a regular time each day to pray together, such as mealtime or bedtime. Ask God to bless your move and your new surroundings. Continue this prayer routine at the new house, and be sure to encourage your children to thank God as he answers their prayers.

* Let your children help. Your children can help with packing by putting their own toys into boxes. Let them decide which favorite toys to keep with them for comfort during the move.

* Maintain established routines. Young children feel more secure when their routines are not interrupted. For example, if breakfast started with a glass of orange juice at the old house, start it the same way at the new house. Children love what is familiar to them, so keep things the same as much as possible.

With just a little care, your children can transition very well in the move.

Vicki Wiley holds a Master of Arts in Theology, with an emphasis on children in crisis, from Fuller Seminary. At present, she is Director of Children's Ministries at First Presbyterian Church in Honolulu, Hawaii.

Spaghetti night was Sam's favorite. Dad made his special sauce. Mom fixed a salad. Jack cooked the pasta. And Sam got to heat the garlic bread in the microwave. Then they all sat down at the table to eat together.

After saying the blessing, everyone shared something about the day. Tonight Jack told about a boy in his fourth-grade class who was teaching him how to juggle. Sam said his best friend, Max, and he were practicing so they could join the soccer team. Mom said she and Dad had some exciting news.

Dad grinned. "I'm getting a new job. And here's the best part . . . we're all moving to California!"

"Isn't that great?" asked Mom.

"Wow!" said Jack. "Can I get a surfboard?"

Sam felt like a little fish was flopping in his tummy. "How far away is California?" he asked.

"Thousands of miles," said Jack. "We learned about it in social studies. It's right by the Pacific Ocean. The sun shines every day. You can go to Disneyland anytime you want, and there are movie stars everywhere. Wait 'til my friends hear!"

"I like it here," said Sam. "We have the lake to swim in and snow in winter. You don't even know any movie stars. Besides, Max and I are going to be on the soccer team next year."

"Well," Dad said, "there's lots of time to talk about it. Now, who wants more spaghetti with my world-famous sauce?"

Sam wasn't very hungry. Jack always liked new things, but Sam liked things the way they were. What if he didn't make any friends in California? What if he didn't know what they were studying at his new school? And what about Max? They had been best friends forever.

That night Jack hung down over the side of his bunk, upside down. "You know what the best part of moving is?"

"No," said Sam. "What?"

"We're each going to get our own room! I can't wait!"

Sam closed his eyes. He couldn't remember not sharing a room with his big brother. He liked knowing Jack was sleeping on the top bunk. He hugged his stuffed bear, Panda. At least Panda would still be with him.

A big tear rolled down the side of Sam's face, right into his ear. He didn't like one thing about moving. Not one thing.

The next day, Sam told Max about moving.

"But what about the soccer team?" Max asked.

"I told Mom and Dad about that," said Sam, "but nobody was listening to me."

"We've been friends forever!" said Max. "I know what! You could stay with us. We could be like brothers. It would be great!"

Sam thought about Max's idea. "I don't know," he said. He liked Max, but he loved his own family too. He didn't want to live at someone else's house. He wanted to stay in his own house, in his own room, with his own family.

Everyone was excited. Dad planned a big garage sale. Jack bought surfing magazines. Mom got maps and pictures off the Internet.

"Look here, Sammy," she said. "Here's your new school. How fun! You get to eat lunch outside at picnic tables!"

"I don't want to eat lunch on a picnic table," Sam said. "I don't want to surf or miss winter or have my own room or leave my friends. I'm going to stay right here and be on the soccer team with Max." Sam crossed his arms, turned around, stomped to his room, and slammed the door.

The bedroom door opened, and Mom sat down beside Sam.

She put her hand on Sam's back and rubbed it in circles. "Sammy, I like things here too; and I know you feel sad about leaving Max."

"Then why do we have to move?" Sam turned over and put his head on Mom's lap.

"Families need to stick together. I know it's scary for you right now, but could you try to be brave? We could ask God for help. How about that?"

"I guess so."

Mom hugged Sam. "Dear Lord, please help each of us to trust you more. And especially show Sam some reasons to feel better about moving."

Moving day finally came. The movers packed up everything in Sam's house then put everything into a huge truck and drove off. Sam went to get his suitcase, and that's when he realized Panda was gone!

"Mom!" he yelled. "Dad! Jack! Has anyone seen Panda?"

No one had. They looked in the house. They looked in the trash bin. They looked all over the yard. Panda wasn't anywhere.

"Maybe he got packed," said Jack.

Sam had a big lump in his throat as they loaded up the car and started off for California.

Dad and Mom took turns driving. Jack and Sam played travel games, like finding alphabet letters on road signs and "I Spy." Dad sang silly songs and told funny stories. Along the way, they stopped to see interesting places like "Cowboy Joe's Buffalo Ranch" and "Dinosaur Park." Sam bought postcards with pictures of dinosaurs to send to Max. Every night Sam missed his bear and prayed that Panda would show up at their new house.

After five days, they arrived in California. Dad drove the car by their new house. It was tan colored and had a red tile roof. There was a tall palm tree growing in the front yard.

"We don't have the keys yet," Mom said. "We're going to stay in a motel until the moving truck brings all our things, and we can move in a few days from now."

Sam thought the house looked okay. As they drove down the street, he saw some kids playing soccer in one of the yards.

A few blocks from the house, they drove by the school.

"This will be your new school, boys," said Dad. "Look at that playground!"

Sam and Jack looked. There was a big blacktopped area with basketball hoops, and a baseball field behind that. There were swings and monkey bars and a big jungle gym too. School didn't start for two weeks. Sam wondered where he would sit for lunch and if anyone would want to play on the monkey bars with him.

Finally, the moving men delivered everything to the new house. Each box was labeled. Sam started tearing open the boxes from his room. He opened box after box, but no Panda.

Jack called down the hall, "Any luck yet?"

"No," Sam said.

"Boy, what a long trip!" a funny voice said.

Sam looked up. Panda was peeking around the corner. Sam spied Jack's hand around the bear.

"Panda!" Sam ran and grabbed his bear. Jack laughed.

"I found him in my bottom dresser drawer," Jack said. "Maybe one of the movers stuck him there so he wouldn't get lost."

It took awhile before everything was unpacked. One day the phone rang. It was Max! Sam told him about their new house and about finding Panda. He told him about the playground at school and about meeting some of the kids who lived nearby.

"But I don't care how many new kids I meet. You'll always be my best friend, Max. Hey, maybe you could come out here to visit. I have my own room now, and there's plenty of space!"

"Yeah," said Max. "And I could bring my soccer ball. We could practice together, just like before."

That night when Sam went to bed, he hugged Panda extra tight and looked out his bedroom window. Then he noticed something.

The moon and the stars looked pretty much the same as they did back at his old house. Some things, he decided, don't change after all.

About the Author

Pamela Kennedy lives in Hawaii with her husband and their crooked-tailed, gray-and-white cat, Gilligan. Three days a week, Pamela teaches at a school for girls in Honolulu. When she's not teaching, she writes. She has loved writing stories ever since she was in elementary school. As the wife of a Naval officer, Pam understands the challenges of moving. She and her family have moved nearly twenty times, ten during her children's younger years.

About the Artist

Anton Petrov was born in Russia but his family moved to South Africa when he was thirteen years old. Upon graduation from the National School of Fine Arts in Johannesburg, Petrov moved to New Zealand. He says: "I always drew pictures. Before I wanted to be a doctor, I remember I really wanted to be a pilot; and before that, my parents say, I wanted to be a builder. The truth is, I always wanted to be an artist." He got his wish.